W9-BGE-900

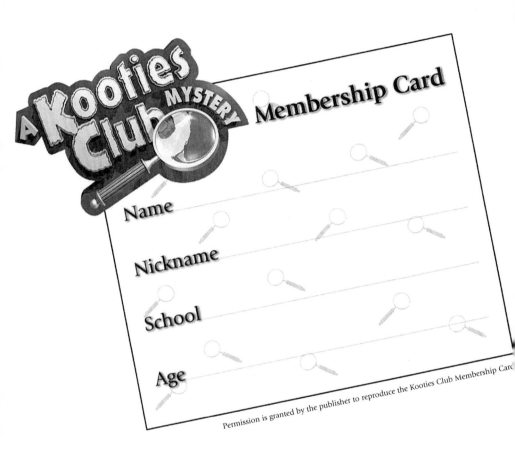

A Kooties Club MYSTERY

Membership Card

Name

Nickname

School

Age

The Mystery of the Old Car

by M. J. Cosson

Perfection Learning®

Cover and Inside Illustrations: Michael A. Aspengren

For information, contact
Perfection Learning® Corporation,
1000 North Second Avenue, P.O. Box 500,
Logan, Iowa 51546-0500.
Tel: 1-800-831-4190
Fax: 1-800-543-2745
www.perfectionlearning.com
PB ISBN-10: 0-7891-6575-9 ISBN-13: 978-0-7891-6575-6
RLB ISBN-10: 0-7569-4606-9 ISBN-13: 978-0-7569-4606-7

7 8 9 10 11 12 PP 20 19 18 17

Table of Contents

Introduction

Abe, Ben, Gabe, Toby, and Ty live in a large city. There isn't much for kids to do. There isn't even a park close by.

Their neighborhood is made up of
apartment houses and trailer parks.
Gas stations and small shops stand
where the parks and grass used to be.
And there aren't many houses with
big yards.

Ty and Abe live in an apartment complex. Next door is a large vacant lot. It is full of brush, weeds, and trash. A path runs across the lot. On the other side is a trailer park. Ben and Toby live there.

Across the street from the trailer park is a big gray house. Gabe lives in the top apartment of the house.

The five boys have known one another since they started school. But they haven't always been friends.

The other kids say the boys have cooties. And the other kids won't touch them with a ten-foot pole. So Abe, Ben, Gabe, Toby, and Ty have formed their own club. They call it the Kooties Club.

Here's how to join. If no one else
will have anything to do with you,
you're in.

The boys call themselves the Koots
for short. Ben's grandma calls his
grandpa an *old coot*. And Ben thinks
his grandpa is pretty cool. So if he's
an old coot, Ben and his friends must
be young koots.

The Koots play ball and hang out
with one another. But most of all,
they look for mysteries to solve.

Chapter 1

The Old Car

The old car sat in the back corner of the apartment parking lot. It had been there for many days. It sat under a tree and beside some bushes. Not many people would see it there.

Long ago, the car had been a beauty. It was big and long. It had huge tail fins that made it look like it could fly.

Now the car's paint was dull. Its tires were old. Its motor barely ran. It cost too much to drive because it used too much gas.

The car's owner who had loved it was dead. The car seemed to be waiting for something. What would happen to it now?

● ● ● ● ● ● ● ● ● ● ● ● ● ● ● ●

The Koots were walking to school. Gabe walked backwards. He couldn't stop looking at the car. It looked like a car from the future and a car from the past.

"That car has been here for days," he said. "I don't think it's moved an inch."

"What car?" Abe asked. Gabe pointed.

"The two-tone," Ty said. He turned around and looked at the car.

"Two-tone?" Abe asked. "How do you know what the horn sounds like?"

"Not the tone of the horn, Abe. The tone of the color. That car is two colors," Gabe said.

"And it has huge tail fins," Ben added.

"Fish have tail fins, not cars," Abe said.

"Stop it," Toby said. "Abe, you're cracking me up."

Abe held his hands out, palms up. "I'm just asking," he said. "How else will I know?"

"Good point," Ben said. "Abe, tail fins are those big things on the back

12

of the car. They were cool a long time ago. So was two-tone."

"It's still cool," Gabe said. "That is a sweet car." The Koots all nodded. They walked back to the car.

"What kind is it?" Ben asked.

"I think it's a Cadillac," Ty said. "My brother puts pictures of old cars all over our bedroom walls. I'm sure it's a Cadillac. It's from the fifties."

"You're good!" Toby said.

Ty smiled. "When you're around my brother, you learn about cars. That's all he talks about."

"We have to go to school," Ben said. "Let's see if it's still here this afternoon."

• • • • • • • • • • • • • • • • • • •

The car was still there.

"See, no one is driving it. It hasn't moved," Gabe said.

"Maybe the person always parks in this same spot," Ben said.

"Do you know how the police tell if a car moves?" Toby asked. "They chalk the tires. I've seem them do it on TV shows."

"What good does that do?" Gabe asked.

"Well, when the car moves, the wheels go around. So you make a chalk mark on a place on the tire. Then, if someone takes the car out and brings it back, the chalk mark is in a different place."

"Let's do it," Ty said. The Koots agreed.

"Who has chalk?" Ben asked.

"My sister has some for writing on the sidewalk," Gabe said.

"Let's go get it!" Toby said.

• • • • • • • • • • • • • • • • •

Half an hour later, the tires had lines of chalk that pointed toward the ground. The next morning when the Koots walked past, the chalk marks were in the same place. They checked for three days, and the car didn't move.

Friday after school, Gabe said, "This car doesn't belong to anybody."

"We don't know that," Toby said.

"I bet it's stolen," Ty said.

"Who would steal such an old car? I think somebody dumped it," Abe said.

Ben checked behind the car. "The license plate is three years old," he said. "This car probably hasn't been

16

driven in years."

"Yes it has," Gabe said. "It hasn't always been here. How else did it get here?"

"This is a mystery," Abe said.

"Yup, and it's a really good mystery because it's about a car!" Ty said.

Chapter 2

Going for a Ride

Saturday morning, the Koots were standing by the car.

Gabe was the first to try the door. It opened! Gabe climbed in the front seat. Then Toby stepped in. Then the other three Koots slid into the back seat.

"Sweet!" Gabe said.

"This car is in good shape," Ben said. "I don't see a hole or a rip in the seats."

"It smells kind of dusty," Abe said. He wrinkled his nose.

"Get over it," Toby said. "It's just old. Roll down the windows. We'll air it out."

"Where shall we go?" Gabe asked.

"We can't go anywhere," Ben said. "We're kids. Anyway, we need a key."

"Well, we can pretend," Gabe said.

"Let's just go for a drive," Toby said. "You know, a test drive."

"Brrrrrrr," Abe blew air through his lips to make a sound like a motor. The other Koots gave him a strange look. But pretty soon they were taking turns making motor sounds.

19

Ben talked about where they were going. "We're pulling out of the parking lot. Now we're going down the street. Oh, stop, Gabe. It's a red light. Okay, now the light is green. Turn right here. Next block, turn left. There's the school. Don't go too fast here. You'll get a ticket. Oh, it's starting to rain. Roll up the windows."

Ty was sitting in the middle of the back seat. When the windows were rolled up again, he began to smell a strange smell.

"Something is wrong," Ty said.

Toby looked at him. "What's wrong?" he asked.

"Something smells," Ty said.

"It's just the dust," Abe said.

"No," Ty said. "It's not just the dust. Something smells rotten."

Suddenly Ty jumped. He leaned across Abe. He opened the back door. He jumped out and ran from the car. He stood a few feet away.

"Get out!" Ty yelled. "There's a dead body in the trunk!"

21

Chapter 3

The Body in the Trunk

The Koots all jumped out of the car. They ran to where Ty was standing.

Ben was the first to speak. "How do you know there's a dead body in the trunk?" he asked.

Ty was shaking. "I just know. I could smell it. Anyway, why else is this car sitting here? Somebody killed somebody else and put the body in the trunk."

"You're nuts," Toby said. "There's no body in that trunk. I didn't smell anything. Did you guys smell it?"

Ben said, "No."

Gabe said, "I don't think so."

Abe said, "Well, maybe. I've seen stuff like that on TV."

"Look guys, this isn't a TV show," Ben said. "Here we have a chance to have a real clubhouse. We can use this car. We can have so much fun in it. Let's not ruin it."

"I'm not playing in a car that has a dead body in the trunk," Ty said.

"It doesn't have a dead body in the trunk," Toby said.

"How do you know?" Ty asked.

"How do you know it does?" Toby asked.

"The smell," Ty said.

"There's no smell!" Ben shouted.

"I know," Gabe said. "If there's a body in the trunk, it will only smell worse tomorrow. Let's come back tomorrow and smell it."

The Koots agreed. They spent the rest of the day playing ball. But they all kept thinking about the old car. And the body that might be in the trunk.

Chapter 4

The Key

Sunday afternoon, the sun was shining. The Koots stood beside the old car. Toby walked back by the trunk. He took a big sniff.

"Smells okay to me," he said.

"Me too," Ben said.

Gabe agreed. "I don't smell anything."

Ty and Abe looked at each other. "Maybe we can smell things other people can't smell," Ty said.

"I don't really smell anything," Abe said.

"Okay," Ty said. "Get back in. But can I sit in the front seat? The back seat smells."

Ty sat in the driver's seat. Abe sat in the other front seat. Toby, Gabe, and Ben sat in back. They rolled the windows down.

Abe pushed the button in front of him. The glove box door popped open. Abe looked inside.

"Look what I found!" Abe shouted. "A state map!" He looked again. Under the map was a key. He held it up. The sun struck it and made it shine.

26

"Wow," Ty said. "Now I can really drive this car."

"You can't drive," Abe said.

"I know," Ty said. "But at least we can lock it. Then no one can take it from us."

"I have an idea," Toby said. "Let's see if the key opens the trunk."

"Good idea," Ben said. "Then we'll know if there really is a body."

Abe held up the key. "I'm not touching that trunk. Who wants to do it?"

"Not me," said Toby, Ty, and Ben.

Gabe shook his head. He took the key. "I'll do it," he said.

All of the Koots climbed out of the car. Gabe walked back to the trunk. He stuck the key in the hole. He turned the key. Slowly the trunk opened.

Gabe screamed.

Chapter 5

A Plan

Gabe fell down. He was rolling on the ground. He was laughing so hard he couldn't stand up.

"I scared you guys," he said. Finally, he sat up. "You should have seen your faces!"

"So there's no body?" Ty asked.

"No, there's no body," Ben said.

He stood up and looked in the trunk. He saw a few tools and a dirty rag.

The other Koots came close to look in the trunk.

"Oh good," Ty said. "Now we can really play in the car and not worry."

Gabe slammed the trunk shut. The Koots climbed back in the car. This time it was Ben's turn to drive. He took the Koots to the Grand Canyon. He pointed out the sights along the way. The trip was very long.

Ben kept saying, "There's another cactus!" But another cactus wasn't enough to make the trip interesting. The Koots were almost asleep.

Suddenly there was a "wham" on the driver's door. The Koots all jumped. Now they were awake.

Mr. Wagner stuck his head in Ben's

window. He was a scary-looking old man. He had thick glasses. They made his eyes look big. His breath smelled like he had been eating onions.

"What do you kids think you're doing?" he shouted. "Don't you know it's dangerous to play in cars? Get out of this car!"

The Koots scrambled out of the car. But Ben was trapped in the front seat. Mr. Wagner still had his head in the window. He was looking around. Ben leaned back against the seat to stay out of Mr. Wagner's way.

"Sir," Ben asked. "Do you know whose car this is?"

Mr. Wagner stared Ben in the eye. He was only a few inches from Ben's face.

"I think I do," Mr. Wagner said. He pulled his head out of the window. He looked at the other Koots standing beside the car. "And you'd better leave it alone. Now go! Scram!"

Mr. Wagner opened the door for Ben. He stood by the car until the Koots had left.

The five Koots walked toward the trailer court.

"Now what?" Toby asked. "We can't play in the car anymore."

Ben held up the key. "We'll go back after dark and lock it up. I don't think Mr. Wagner really knows whose car it is. I think he wants it for himself."

"We're going to lose that car," Toby said.

"Unless we can find out who it belongs to," Ty said.

"What good will that do?" Ben asked.

"Well, maybe they'll let us play in it. They don't seem to want it anyway. We're careful. We won't start the car. We won't get in trouble," Gabe said.

"If Mr. Wagner knows whose car it is, he might offer them money," Ben said. "We don't have any money to offer. We need a plan."

"I have an idea," Ty said. "Let's ask my brother. He knows all about cars. He might know what to do."

The Koots did the Kootie handshake on Ty's idea. It was the best idea they had. It was the only idea.

Chapter 6

Who Has the Key?

After dark, Ty's brother Jack came back to the old car with the Koots.

"Awesome!" he said when he saw the car. "Why didn't you tell me about this before?" he asked Ty.

"Because it's our car," Ty said.

"Oh? How is it your car?" Jack asked.

"We found it," Ty said.

"Finders keepers," Abe added.

"It doesn't belong to anybody," Gabe said.

"This car belongs to somebody," Jack said. He opened the car's hood. He looked at the motor. "It's in great shape. With just a little work, it would be worth a lot of money. I bet someone is storing it here."

"So how do we find out?" Ben asked.

Jack climbed inside the car. He looked in the glove box. He looked under the seats. "Were there any papers here?"

"Nope," the Koots all said together.

Jack climbed out and opened the trunk. Then he saw the license plate. "I can find out who owns this car," he

36

said. Jack pulled a pen from his jeans pocket. He wrote down the license plate number on his hand. Then he said, "Give me the key."

"Why?" Ty asked.

"So I can lock it up," Jack said.

"We'll lock it up," Ben said.

"Do you want my help?" Jack asked.

The Koots looked at each other. They nodded.

"Then give me the key," Jack said again. "I'll lock it up. I'll keep the key. I'll find out whose car this is."

Ben handed Jack the key. Jack locked the car and put the key in his pocket. As he walked away, he called back to the Koots. "Thanks, guys. You did the right thing."

"That doesn't make me feel any better," Gabe said.

"We might as well have given the key to Mr. Wagner," Toby said.

"Great idea, Ty," Ben said.

"Sorry, guys," Ty said. "I thought he'd be more helpful."

"Do you know what?" Abe asked. "He is doing just what we asked him to."

"Yeah," Ty said. "But I didn't plan that he would keep the key."

Gabe looked at Ty. "Can you get the key back from him after he's asleep tonight?"

"Not tonight," Ty said. "He stays up too late. But maybe in the morning I can take the key from his pants pocket before he wakes up."

38

Chapter 7

New York City

After school the next day, the Koots were sitting in the old car. Ty had taken the key from Jack's pants pocket that morning. Then he took the key to school. Jack hadn't had a chance to take the key back.

Toby was driving them around New York City. He had never been to New York City, so he was making a lot of it up.

"There's the Statue of Liberty," Toby pointed out the window.

The Koots all looked where Toby was pointing. But they didn't see the Statue of Liberty. They saw Jack walking across the parking lot. A lady was with him. She was using a walker. The Koots stared. No one said anything. They just watched Jack and the lady slowly move closer.

"Hi, guys. I thought I might find you here," Jack said. "I found the owner. The county had her old address and phone number. She still has the same phone number, so here she is. This is Mrs. Rosen. Mrs. Rosen, this is my brother Tyrone and his friends."

"Hi," the Koots all said.

40

Mrs. Rosen nodded. "I'm glad you boys are taking good care of Alice," she said.

The Koots looked surprised.

"We named the car Alice," Mrs. Rosen added. "Oh, how my husband loved Alice. But I'm afraid I'm going to have to sell her now."

"How did it get here? I mean how did she get here?" Abe asked.

"I drove Alice here a month ago," Mrs. Rosen said. "I used to live in a big, old house not far from here. Alice was in the garage. It was time for me to sell the house and move to an apartment. The car hadn't been driven for years, but I drove her here and parked her. I'm surprised we made it. Old Alice wasn't in very good shape, and I hadn't driven in years. The movers brought my other things in a van."

Mrs. Rosen smiled. "Alice had been my husband's second love. He took very good care of her. I really hate to sell Alice, but I have no use for her anymore. I do have some nice memories."

42

"Would you like to sit down?" Toby asked.

Ben got out of the back seat and stood beside Jack. Mrs. Rosen got in.

"Where were you just driving to?" she asked Toby.

"New York City," Toby said.

"Oh, I love New York City," Mrs. Rosen said. "I used to live there. In fact, we bought Alice when we moved here from New York in 1959."

"Wow," the Koots all said together.

"We knew this car was old, but that's really old!" Abe said.

"Yes," Mrs. Rosen said. "We were all young back then—my husband, Alice, and I."

43

Mrs. Rosen sat quietly for a minute. Then she tapped Toby on the shoulder. "Could you take us for a ride, young man?" she asked.

"Not really," Toby said. "But I can pretend."

"You drive and I'll tell you where we are in New York City," Mrs. Rosen said.

The Koots all sat back. Jack and Ben leaned against the outside. Mrs. Rosen took them down Fifth Avenue. She took them through Central Park. She took them to Wall Street. Mrs. Rosen took the Koots all through New York City. And when the Koots closed their eyes, it was almost as if they were really there.

Mrs. Rosen ended the ride by taking them over the George

44

Washington Bridge to New Jersey.

When she was done, Mrs. Rosen said, "Well, boys, this has been wonderful. I'm so glad this old car finally had some company. Poor Alice had been sitting alone in the garage since my husband died. This was a very nice farewell party for her.

"Now I need to put an ad in the paper and sell her," Mrs. Rosen added.

Jack leaned in the window. "I have an idea, Mrs. Rosen," he said.

Mrs. Rosen looked up.

Jack went on, "I take classes at a trade school. We are learning to fix cars. We work on old cars some of the time. I could take Alice to school, and we could work on her. Then you could sell her for more money."

Mrs. Rosen smiled.

"We would paint Alice and fix the motor," Jack said. "We would put on new tires. You would have to pay a little for our work, but you would make a lot more money if the car looked good and ran well."

Now Mrs. Rosen had a huge smile on her face. "Oh, that would be lovely!" she said.

Chapter 8

Alice's Makeover

A month later, all five Koots were stuffed into Alice's wide back seat. Jack was driving. Mrs. Rosen sat in the other front seat.

"She's beautiful, Jack!" Mrs. Rosen said. "And she runs so smoothly!" It was about the fifth time she had said that.

Alice had a shiny new coat of paint. Jack and his classmates had taken her motor apart. Then they had put it all back together again. Alice had new tires.

This ride was to show off Alice to her friends. It was also a good-bye ride. Alice was about to be sold.

"How are you going to sell Alice, Mrs. Rosen?" Ben asked.

"I'm going to put an ad in the paper," Mrs. Rosen said. "I don't know how many people will want to buy an old car. Yes, she looks great, but she uses a lot of gas."

"Collectors will want her," Jack said. "They won't drive her much. They'll just keep her for car shows. You should get a lot of money for her."

Mrs. Rosen looked at Jack. "Money is nice, but I'd rather know that Alice is being taken care of."

"Oh, a collector will take good care of her, Mrs. Rosen," Jack said.

"I wish I could buy her," Gabe said.

"Me too," Ty said.

"And me," Toby said.

"And me," Abe said.

"Me too," Ben said.

Mrs. Rosen looked back at the boys. "I wish I could just give you the car, but I am not rich," she said.

Jack looked at Mrs. Rosen. "My teacher collects cars. He really likes Alice. I wonder if he would buy her. Then you would know where she is."

Mrs. Rosen smiled. "I'll go ahead

and put the ad in the paper. What will be, will be."

• • • • • • • • • • • • • • • • •

Two days later, the Koots were all sitting on Gabe's front steps. Jack drove up in Alice. He stopped and got out of the car.

"I have some good news for you guys," Jack said. "I'm buying Alice."

"What!" Ty said. "How can you afford to?"

Jack smiled. "Mrs. Rosen is letting me make payments on the car. I pay Mrs. Rosen something every month. Alice will be all mine in three years!"

"Let me ask my question again," Ty said. "How can you afford to?"

"I made a really good deal," Jack said. "I pay Mrs. Rosen every month. I

50

also take her to the store every week in Alice. I also have to take you guys somewhere every month."

"Yeah!" the Koots said.

"That's part of the deal?" Toby asked.

"Yes," Jack said. "But there's a catch. You have to pay for the gas. That means if you want me to take you across town, it will cost lots of money. If you'll settle for just riding to the store with Mrs. Rosen, it won't cost you a cent. That will be up to you."

"So you'll drive Alice to school?" Ty asked.

"No," Jack said. "I can't afford to drive Alice anywhere. She is a way for me to save money. As she gets older,

she will be worth even more money. If I ever need to sell her, I will make a lot of money. I also might use her to make money. I can drive people to special places. I could take people to the prom or to weddings. They would pay me."

"So, if we want a ride in Alice, we have to pay you?" Ty asked.

"Right," Jack said.

Ty looked at Abe, Toby, Ben, and Gabe. They all smiled.

"We'll go to the store with Mrs. Rosen!" they said.

Chapter 9

Alice All Over Again

A few days later, the Koots were walking home from school. They saw an old car parked on the street. They walked toward the car. It wasn't as nice as Alice. But it was old. It looked like it had been sitting on the street for a long time.

"I bet somebody dumped this car," Toby said.

"It doesn't look like it's been driven for a long time," Ben said.

Ty tried the door. The car was unlocked. Ty got in. Then Toby, Abe, Gabe, and Ben got in.

"Where shall we go?" Ty asked.

"How about to Las Vegas?" Toby said.

"What's there?" Abe asked.

"I don't know. Lights, I guess," Toby said.

The Koots rolled down all the windows.

"Let's go to Chicago," Gabe said. "Maybe another Mrs. Rosen will come along and tell us about the city."

"Okay, Chicago," Ty said. "I don't know anything about Chicago."

Suddenly a man opened Ty's door. "What are you kids doing in my car? Scram!" he yelled.

The Koots jumped out of the car and ran down the street. The man was yelling at them.

"Next time I'll call the police. Stay out of people's cars!"

The Koots ran for two blocks. They all fell down in Gabe's front yard. Everyone was laughing hard.

"I guess I won't be getting into any more strange cars!" Abe said.

After they were done laughing, the Koots all lay on the ground. They looked up at the trees and the clouds.

Finally Toby sat up. "Okay, Koots," he said. "We're done with cars for now. Let's go find another mystery to solve!"